WHO WOKE THE BABY?

For my baby granddaughter, Angelina
J.C.

For Fred
C.F.

First published in 2015 by Nosy Crow Ltd

The Crow's Nest, 10a Lant Street

London SE1 1QR

www.nosycrow.com

ISBN 978 0 85763 408 5 (HB)

ISBN 978 0 85763 409 2 (PB)

Nosy Crow and associated logos are trademarks
and/or registered trademarks of Nosy Crow Ltd.

Text copyright © Jane Clarke 2015

Illustrations copyright © Charles Fuge 2015

The right of Jane Clarke to be identified as the author of this work
and of Charles Fuge to be identified as the illustrator of this work has been asserted.

A CIP catalogue record for this book is available from the British Library.

Printed in China by Imago

Papers used by Nosy Crow are made from wood grown in sustainable forests.

1 3 5 7 9 8 6 4 2 (HB)

1 3 5 7 9 8 6 4 2 (PB)

WHO WOKE THE BABY?

Jane Clarke

Illustrated by Charles Fuge

nosy crow

This is the **baby**

that woke at dawn,

smelly and **yelly**

and all forlorn.

This is the **hippo** that yawned a **yawn**

that woke the baby up at dawn,

smelly and **yelly** and all forlorn.

This is the **zebra** that made a **fuss**

that woke up Hippopotamus

who yawned a goofy, toothy **yawn**

that woke the baby up at dawn,

smelly and **yelly** and all forlorn.

This is the **lion** with **pointy** claws

that woke up Zebra with his **roars.**

No wonder Zebra made a **fuss**

that woke up Hippopotamus

who yawned a goofy, toothy **yawn**

that woke the baby up at dawn,

smelly and **yelly** and all forlorn.

This is the **crocodile**, all **snappy**,
that woke up Lion, so unhappy
that Lion **snarled** and showed his claws
and woke up Zebra with his **roars**.

No wonder Zebra made a **fuss**

that woke up Hippopotamus

who yawned a goofy, toothy **yawn**

that woke the baby up at dawn,

smelly and **yelly** and all forlorn.

This is the **frog** that croaked a **croak**
so **loud** that Crocodile awoke.
He thrashed about, all **snippy-snappy**
and woke up Lion, so unhappy
that Lion **snarled** and showed his claws
and woke up Zebra with his **roars.**

No wonder Zebra made a **fuss**

that woke up Hippopotamus

who yawned a goofy, toothy **yawn**

that woke the baby up at dawn,

smelly and **yelly** and all forlorn.

This is the **bee,** all **stripy** and **fuzzy**
that woke up Frog by being so **buzzy.**
Bee **buzzed** and made Frog croak a **croak**
so **loud** that Crocodile awoke.
He thrashed about, all **snippy-snappy**
and woke up Lion, so unhappy . . .

. . . that Lion **snarled** and showed his claws

and woke up Zebra with his **roars.**

No wonder Zebra made a **fuss**

that woke up Hippopotamus

who yawned a goofy, toothy **yawn**

that woke the baby up at dawn.

Poor little
Baby,
all forlorn.

This is the
beautiful
butterfly . . .

... that **fluttered**

through the dawning sky
and touched down gently, as you see,
on a flower with busy Bee.

Bee **buzzed** and made Frog croak a **croak**
so **loud** that Crocodile awoke.

He thrashed about, all **snippy-snappy**

and woke up Lion, so unhappy

that Lion **snarled** and showed his claws

and woke up Zebra with his **roars.**

No wonder Zebra made a **fuss**

that woke up Hippopotamus

who yawned a goofy, toothy **yawn**

that woke the baby up at dawn.

This is the **baby**
that woke at dawn,
wriggly and **giggly**,
no longer forlorn.

This is the baby,
full of **delight**,
watching the butterfly
dance in the light.

This is the baby,
all **smiling** and **clappy**.
A **new** day has dawned
and **everyone's** happy.